This book belongs to

_____

Written by Emily Gale

Illustrated by Mike Byrne

This edition published by Parragon Books Ltd in 2015

Parragon Books Ltd
Chartist House
15–17 Trim Street
Bath BA1 1HA, UK
www.parragon.com

ISBN 978-1-4723-7725-8

Printed in China

JUST JOSIE

and the lucky number

7

PaRragon

Bath • New York • Cologne • Melbourne • Delhi
Hong Kong • Shenzhen • Singapore • Amsterdam

This is
JOSEPHINE EMILY,
but everyone
just calls her

Josie.

She likes rainbows,
chocolate and Duck

(who is as old as Josie).

a b c

She does NOT like
Zac from next door.
because he is a show-off.

milk
bread
eggs
cheese

This is a picture
of Zac showing off
and Josie not being
impressed one little bit.

josie

"Isn't that the cleverest thing you've ever seen?" says Zac. "Ner-ner, bet you wish YOU had a dog."

"It's not fair!"

Josie yells and runs up to her bedroom...

... and grabs her paper and pens.

DEEP BREATH,
COUNT TO TEN.
JOSIE'S GOT A
BIG IDEA AGAIN.

I might not have a dog. but I HAVE got a little sister. I'll show Zac what clever tricks REALLY are.

She writes Zac a note.

Dir Zac,
My sista is better
than yor dog.
I will show you
tmorro.   JoSIE.

Josie posts the note underneath
Zac's fence and hurries back inside
to start her Big Idea.

PROJECT LILY

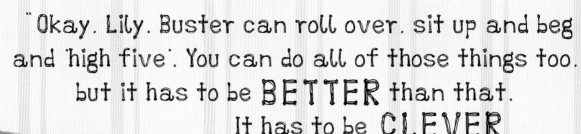

"Okay, Lily. Buster can roll over, sit up and beg
and 'high five'. You can do all of those things too,
but it has to be **BETTER** than that.
It has to be **CLEVER**.
Say the alphabet," says Josie.

Lily takes a deep breath
and talks really loud and fast.

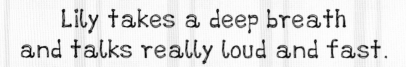

a b c d e f g h i j k
j j j k j j j... k...

And then she stops.
"The alphabet has too many
letters," says Josie.
"I need to find something
easier for you."

"Lily, count to ten," says Josie. Lily starts to spin round and round.

"One... two... three... four... five... six..."

Lily keeps spinning but she stops counting.

"Keep going!" says Josie.

"EIGHT...
NINE...
TEN!"

Lily falls in a heap giggling.

"You missed seven! Try again - this has to be PERFECT to teach that silly old Zac a lesson."

A note has come under the kitchen door.
It is from Zac.

Josie,

Evryone knows that dogs do betta trix.

U R A sor looza.

Zac

Josie CANNOT let Zac think that he can teach better tricks than she can. She is going to teach Lily how special and important the number seven is. "Seven days in the week." she says.

Monday,
Tuesday,
Wednesday,
Thursday,
Friday,
Saturday,
Sunday.

Lily sticks out her tongue. "Seven colours in the rainbow." says Josie. "Red. orange. yellow. green. blue. indigo. violet. Now you try."

Lily grins. "One. two. three. four. five. six. eight. nine. ten!"

and burps.

Josie picks up the beater of her xylophone.
"Seven notes in a scale," she says,
and then Josie sings:

re, mi, fa, so, la, ti."

Lily claps her big sister.

"Say seven. **SE-VEN,**" says Josie. Lily shrugs and says she's hungry.

DEEP BREATH,
COUNT TO TEN.
JOSIE'S GOT A
BIG IDEA AGAIN.

"Zac gives Buster
doggy treats." she says.
"I just need to find
some Lily treats!"

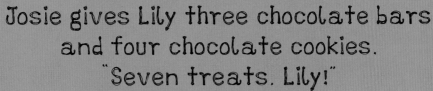

Josie gives Lily three chocolate bars
and four chocolate cookies.
"Seven treats. Lily!"

Lily eats
them really
fast.

She has
chocolate
oozing
out of the
corners
of her
mouth.

She still won't
say seven.

That night Lily watches her big sister button up her pyjamas.

"I'm not speaking to you," says Josie. "You ruined my Big Idea."

Josie cuddles
up to Duck and
won't give Lily
a goodnight kiss.

But later, in the dark, Josie gets a bad feeling all over. She creeps across the floor to where her little sister is sound asleep. Josie loves the way that Lily smells like cupcakes when she's cosy in bed.

"You're still the best sister in the world," she whispers. "Even if you're no good at tricks." Josie gives her sister some goodnight kisses.

"Kisses for your
eyes - one. two.
Nose - three.
Mouth - four.
Cheeks - five. six.
Night-night. Lil."
Then Josie tiptoes away.

And a very sleepy voice says "Seven".
"What did you say?" says Josie.
"Seven." whispers Lily.

One two three four
five six SEVEN
eight nine ten.

Josie climbs into bed with her little sister.
"I don't care what Zac thinks," says Josie.
"You really are BETTER than a dog."

And Lily falls fast asleep in her big sister's arms.